The Simples Love a Picnic

Mom

Dad

Lulu

Ben

Rocco

Dizzy

J. C. Phillipps

Houghton Mifflin Harcourt • Boston New York

To Michael, You are the bread and the knife.

www.hmhbooks.com

The text of this book is set in Berhard.
The illustrations are cut paper.

Library of Congress Cataloging-in-Publication Data
is on file.

ISBN 978-0-544-16667-7

Manufactured in China
SCP 10 9 8 7 6 5 4 3 2 1
4500451962

"Let's have a picnic," says Dad.
Ben tugs on Mom's arm. "What's a picnic?"
Mom smiles. "A picnic is when you pack food in a basket,
spread out a blanket, and eat on the ground."

"Can Rocco come?"
asks Ben.
"Yes," says Dad. "I'll get
his leash."

"Can Dizzy come?"
asks Lulu.
"No," says Dad. "Cats
and picnics don't mix."

Lulu thinks, *This is unfair.*
Lulu has a very big backpack.

Ben wonders, *What kinds of food do you eat at a picnic?*

Cereal?

Spaghetti?

Soup?

Eggs?

Mom says, "You eat foods that don't spill."
Mom packs apples and sandwiches.

Ice cream doesn't spill.

The Simples walk to the park.
Dad carries the blanket.
Lulu carries her big backpack.
Mom carries the picnic basket.

Ben walks Rocco, and . . .

Dad carries the blanket.
Lulu carries her big backpack.
Ben carries the picnic basket.
Mom walks Rocco.

Lulu sings a simple tune, and . . .

Lulu carries the blanket.
Ben carries the picnic basket.
Mom walks Rocco.

Dad takes Dizzy home.

"Cats and picnics don't mix."

The Simples are at the park. Yay!
Where should they sit?

Ben finds a spot.
Uh-oh. Too many ants.

Lulu finds a spot.
Uh-oh. Too many birds.

Mom finds a spot.
Uh-oh. Too many sports.

Dad is back. Yay!
Dad finds the perfect spot.

What a beautiful day!

Mom hands out sandwiches.
Ben eats an apple.

Lulu opens the ice cream.

OH NO!

Do you know who loves

melted

ice

cream?

Oh, no. Looks like there's no picnic for the Simples.
Dad carries Dizzy.
Mom walks Rocco.
Lulu carries the picnic basket.
Ben brings the blanket.

Ben remembers,
*A picnic is when you pack food in a basket,
spread out a blanket,
and eat on the ground.*

Ben has an idea.